All characters in this book are fictional
and any resemblance to any other person, living or dead
is pure coincidence.

Honest!

LAW TO LEATHER:

THE DIARY OF MISS 'DON'T' GOLIGHTLY

The Interview

6th August 2013

Victoria Golightly is sitting in the plush 2nd floor office of Messrs Weston and Weston, a successful family law firm built up by two brothers: Julian and Joseph Weston.   Julian is the elder by two years and slightly more senior.   After a re-organisation within the firm, a vacancy has arisen for a junior associate with a view to eventually becoming a partner.   There are three people in the room: the brothers and Miss Golightly.   The interview is almost at its conclusion and with glowing references from notable members of the law society, the partners feel positive that they have the ideal candidate in front of them.

Julian Weston: Well, Miss Golightly, I feel that the interview is almost concluded unless, Mr Weston, do you have any further questions for Miss Golightly?

Joseph Weston: No, I can't think of anything.

Julian Weston: Well, I have just one last question.   What have you been up to for the last six months?   Your resume doesn't appear to account for the period.

Miss Golightly: Oh, that's when I lost my Grandma.   It was a very difficult time, very traumatic.

Julian Weston: Oh, I totally understand, say no more.   Mr Weston and I felt exactly the same when we lost our dear Grandmother.   And so unexpected too.   One day here and the next day gone.   Died in her sleep.   So sudden.   So tragic.

Both men sentimentally shake their heads

Miss Golightly: Oh she didn't die.   Like I said, I lost her.   It was my turn to visit; Wednesday's my day and, as it happened, one Wednesday in March, I had to go into town, so I took her with me. Well I had to pop into *Ann Summers* to get a few bits and pieces and I couldn't really take her in there, could I?   She's 79 and been a widow for nearly twenty years!   So I left her outside, while I went in and she only wandered off.   Met up with an old bingo pal, Rosie Danks, decided to go off and have a coffee with her didn't she?   To be honest with you, she's getting a bit forgetful, is Grandma. Didn't think to wait for me or even let me know she was off.   It's not like I was in there for long, just had to get a few pieces of equipment and things are quite reasonable in that shop.   Better than some of the
shops round the city centre, anyway.   It's incredible how quickly things get worn out, particularly with over-use and I've been quite busy these last few weekends.

The brothers look at Miss Golightly with puzzled faces

Miss Golightly: Oops, probably shouldn't have said anything, me and my big mouth.   Well it's too late now; I'm a dominatrix at weekends.   In fact I'm Miss Don't Golightly then and I'm always very busy; demand is high.   If I've learnt one thing, it's that all high flyers need to let of steam at the weekend.   Anyway, when I eventually left the shop, there was no sign of Grandma.   Had to search for her and when she didn't return home, we had to send out a search party.   She'd only gone on holiday with this Rosie woman and her toyboy, honestly, the whole thing was quite a trauma and to top it all, my family blamed me.

Julian Weston: Do you not think that this erm…. other job might get in the way of this one?

Miss Golightly: No way, not at all.   I'm very professional. I've been doing it for so long now and I'm very discreet.   Actually, I recognized one or two of my clients while I waited in reception. *As she says this, Miss Golightly taps the side of her nose with her index finger and gives a knowing nod.*

Julian Weston: Well, thank you for coming in today.   *He moves quickly To the door and opens it for Miss Golightly.*

Joseph Weston: Erm, who did you say --?

Julian Weston: --Sorry but time is pressing on and we have lots of other applicants to see…..we'll be in touch!

Julian Weston hurries Miss Golightly out of the interview room, making sure to avoid all physical contact.

*****

The Diary

28th February 1996

Been at Leicester School of Law for 6 months and would like to say I'm learning loads!!! Only joking, haha.   Have decided to be professional and keep a diary though.   Remember having one when I was little but now training to be a top class ever-so-important lawyer, thought it'd be a good idea.   Nothing to do with the fact that I missed a lecture last week due to a hangover from partying Tuesday night!   Law school's not like university, you don't get many parties, everyone's soo serious! So of course, when the chance of a piss up came along….. If I'd had a diary then though, I would've known about important lecture next day and would have left earlier (and drank less). Anyway, diary, 'Welcome to the crazy world of Victoria Golightly!'

29th February 1996

Oh Wow, a leap year day. Does squeezing an extra day into the year, make the planet turn differently? It's not something I've ever thought about before, half expected some kind of phenomenon to occur, like the sky falling down as in *Chicken Licken*, but no, nothing happened –quite boring really.
And to think, I could've proposed to my boyfriend, today, not that I've got one to propose to anyway and I'm not the type of girl who'd just go up to any old guy and ask for his hand in marriage – God no! Then again, there's always the sexy maintenance guy who comes and repairs the house after student parties – he's winked at me a few times, (he also winks at Sheila and Geraldine, for that matter!) - he's probably already spoken for anyway, oh well, there's no harm in looking.

30th March 1996

Damn! Can't believe I've forgotten to fill my diary in, still trying to get used having one in the first place. Must insert completion of diary into my routine.
Oh God it's sooo boring in class at the moment. Studying history of law and lecturer Mr Thompson is such a drag. DON'T KNOW IF I CAN STAND ANOTHER MINUTE!!! Had to write 800 word essay on why I chose law. That was easy enough – chose law because poor father injured back at work and had to leave due to incapacitation. Has had fight on his hands to get compensation from company, who are refusing to accept liability, and I thought that if I had an in depth understanding of the law, I could help my dad. Also, I couldn't see myself as a teacher. There, rounded it up in 60 words – spent rest of class doodling and gawping out of

window at hunky lads playing football on field– not sure if Mr Thompson was impressed though!

Oh well, Easter holidays soon and going back home, I can't wait!

1st April 1996

All fool's day – ah, a day dedicated to me, how sweet.

Hello dear diary, do not stress, I've decided that from now on, I'll spare you the boring details.   In other words, all the interesting stuff, I'll tell you about and all the crap stuff - lessons, notes etc can go in the back of my exercise book.   Great idea.   That way, when I'm old (about 40) and reading about my life in my student days, I won't be bored to death with lecture times, (because who will care then?   I won't because I'll be a top lawyer with my own firm). And I'll be soooo jealous of myself going to loads of parties and fun student stuff!!!

10th April 1996

Got back home (Birmingham) last night, train delayed – as usual, dad met me from the station – as usual, weather's crap – as usual. Went to town with Sara (today) – sisters' shopping trip.   Treated myself to *Erasure* and *Annie Lennox* CD's, Sara bought a new handbag.   We went for lunch in *The Windsor,* shared a bottle of wine, then couldn't be bothered to carry on shopping so stayed there for the remainder of the afternoon and had more wine, got home, missed tea and went straight to bed, don't think dad was impressed but was lovely catching up with sister.

12th October 1996

12th October?   Might as well be 12th of never.   Can't believe I forgot diary again.   Am I hopeless or what?   Anyway, back at law school for final year and it's going to be a hard one, or so I've been told.   Only doing 2 days at college and rest of time split between

placements at Citizen's Advice Bureau and a legal aid centre–
should be interesting.

15th October 1996

I don't think I'm very good with this diary business but I'm doing
my best. But guess what?   Diary, dear diary, I'm in love!   His
name's Simon and he's in my Law and the Community class.   He
has the brightest blue eyes and he keeps looking at me and smiling.
I think he's going to ask me out!!!

19th October 1996

CRAP, CRAP, CRAP, I'M FUMING!! That Simon wasn't
interested in me at all.   He was smiling at that bloody Trisha who
sits next to me.   THE COW!!   She's not even interesting, goes on
and on about her knobby Dad all the time.
'My Father is a top judge and BLAH BLAH SODDING BLAH!'
Oh well, stuff them.   They're welcome to each other. He's probably
a selfish bastard anyway.
Sorry diary, but recent events have caused me to start swearing
again, I must make an effort to stop – I'm not like that!

25th October 1996

Went to student union bar to see a band called The Whizz.   They
weren't very good - could whiz off for all I care! But there was a
great crowd there so I had a good laugh and quite a few drinks.

5th November 1996

Bugger.   Tried to dye my hair blonde and it's gone bloody orange!
That's orange – bloody hell, rather than the red fleshed fruit.   Going

to a Bonfire Party tonight, they'll think I'm in fancy dress as a firework!

In case I am reading this when I'm in my forties and grey - my natural hair colour is darkish brown, which matches my hazel eyes and while we're on the subject of me in my early twenties, I'm five foot, five inches, size 10-12, fit nicely into 34C bras (though manage to squeeze into pretty 34A bra which was £1.99 in the sale, but was on 34C hanger and I couldn't be bothered to take it back).   I prefer *Dorothy Perkins* to *Marks and Spencer* and lost my virginity to Dawn Freeman's boyfriend, David, when I was 16 and at my best friend Mandy's 17th birthday party.   I wonder if Dawn and David are still together!

6th November 1996

Very hung over and had to call in sick to CAB – what a liar!!! Bonfire party was fab.   Met great guy, can't quite remember him but think his name was Nathan, or Neil or something like that.   But he loved my hair!

9th November 1996

Seeing Matthew later, we're going for a drink at the student union bar.   Matthew doesn't begin with an 'N', where did I get that idea from?!

24th November 1996

Mom phoned with bad news, dad's not good at the moment.   Was busy dreaming about new boyfriend, Vicky 'Heart' Matt, and all that kind of stuff, now busy worrying about dad.

25th November 1996

Can't believe it's only a month till Christmas!   Looking forward to going home and seeing my family though.   Hope dad feels better soon.

Must phone Sara and see what she's getting parents for Christmas. Finding course quite intense now and v. hard work, I know I can do it, but….?

26th November 1996

So sorry diary, was I depressing yesterday or what?!   But I'm not today! Saw my wonderful fella last night.   We went for a curry in the town centre.   Had a lovely time and he's a real cutie-pie!

*****

14th April 1998

I DON'T BELIEVE IT!   I've got a job at Cavendish, Crawford and Simpson!   Big law firm in Birmingham.   Junior staff position to start with but who knows where that will lead?   I just knew that voluntary job at the Citizen's Advice would come in handy.   Must go to town and kit oneself out with office clothes – will have to ask mom for a loan.

16th April 1998

Job sorted, now must concentrate on finding a new boyfriend (especially before next leap year, when I can propose– unless he proposes first!!!)   Why do men walk into my life and then sprint out, again?

11th May 1998

First day at work.   It was v. posh but the staff seem friendly enough.   Debbie – receptionist on my floor - is very friendly and showed me the ropes.   Didn't see any of the big knobs today, no doubt they'll show their faces soon enough!

20th May 1998

2nd week at work, seems to be going smoothly.   Caught sight of Mr Simpson, today.   The old git walks like he's got a broom handle stuck up his backside – definitely a knob!   (Oops, must remember language, and manners).

18th August 1998

You know when you're AT WORK when you're IN WORK on your birthday.
No lie-in today, up at seven just like any other working day – oh well, I'm a trainee lawyer now, the carefree days of studenthood and long summer holidays are well and truly behind me.
There were three birthday cards on my desk, when I got in and Debbie and Pippa – from filing – insisted that we all went for a drink, after work.   Went to the *James Brindley* – love it in there, but was home by nine on account of it being a Tuesday – as opposed to it being a Friday.   Oh goodie, I've only got to wait until I'm 26 to go and get pissed on my birthday!

19th August 1998

No hangover today and back to work – how normal and boring everything is when you're working.   Mandy said she's taking me to lunch on Friday – she's finally got a day off!

9th November 1998

Was called into Nicholas Crawford's office today.   Was crapping myself but it was ok.   They like my work and have given me a small caseload to work on with Molly, the other 'new girl.' She seems ok. Here comes the high life! In fact Nicholas Crawford is quite nice too!

16th November 1998

YUK! Had to go to prison – in a professional capacity, not to live. Assisted Nicholas Crawford with a case he's working on. Peter Bulliver the toothbrush stealer – yes, honest. He's got this thing about toothbrushes and can't go into a shop without robbing the lot from the shelf, apparently. You wouldn't think it to look at the state of his teeth, though. He spent the whole interview staring at my chest.
'Oi, matey, my face is up here,' I wanted to say, but restrained myself.
There were times I really wanted to laugh but can't – I have to look professional. (I've started practicing my '*Now you're in a lot of trouble, mate,*' look, when I'm near a mirror.)
The prison stinks and I couldn't get out quick enough but it was interesting, I hate to admit. I think I have to go back tomorrow. At least I had the delightful Nicholas Crawford showing me the ropes. He can show me anything he likes!

17th November 1998

Dad's depression is back and mom's tearing her hair out. We're all rallying round to try and help. Sara's come back from uni for a while to help, it's great having sis home again, even though there's this huge black cloud hanging over the house. At least I'm at work in the day. Mom's threatening to go back to full-time work – which will be really crap because then I'll have to do my own washing and ironing. I'm trying not to be selfish here but I can't help it. He always seems to get so much worse in the winter.

21st November 1998

Oh God, mom's at her wits end.   They're going to Relate, what if they get divorced?   Me and Sara will be from a broken home? No, seriously, I am scared.   I don't want my parents to split up, they were childhood sweethearts and on the subject of which, I'm still boyfriend-less.   Must make an effort to sort out my love-life, especially now I'm settled in an important but demanding career. Splashed out and spent a tenner on the lottery, a million quid would've sorted everything – won naff all.

7th December 1998

It's pretty crap at home.   Mom and dad have decided to separate but they both seem ok about it and dad doesn't seem so depressed anymore – 'Err, hello, nobody asked me how I feel about it.' Seriously, I hope they'll be alright.
On a lighter note, me and Molly have been put in charge of the junior solicitor's part of the Cavendish, Crawford and Simpson Christmas Party.   How groovy is that?   They usually have it in a hall but they've decided to hold it in the office this year.
'Probably to save money,' Christina said.
Snooty cow.   What does she know?
'They probably just want to have somewhere they can spend the night if they get too hammered; those couches in reception look dead comfy!' I said.
'You wouldn't see me sleeping on an office couch,' the snooty cow said and I had visions of her struggling to get comfy on twenty mattresses and a pea.

14th December 1998

I CAN'T BELIEVE IT!   The office party's Friday night but I have to spend the day at that bloody prison!!!   I can't go there in my party clothes, they'll think I am a right tart!   DAMN DAMN DAMN!

15th December 1998

It's fine, it's cool, everything's groovy.   Nick (that's what he's told me to call him, quite sexy I think), said I can use the shower in the knob's bathroom when I get back from the smelly prison so I can get myself dolled up for the party, which I'm really looking forward to. And I picked up a right bargain dress from *Miss Selfridge*, at the weekend.   Low-cut, gold and glittery and only 30 quid!

17th December 1998

HOORAH! Almost done my time at the prison - for now.   Don't have to go again till next year - thank God.   Have finished that part of my training according to Steven Cavendish, so PHEW!
Got a new case though, some crusty old toff on a sex charge.   Been caught lifting women's skirts to look at their underwear, whenever and wherever he gets the chance.   WHAT A PERV!   He did it to some woman in a shop and then stood under the stairs and watched her walk up and it turned out she was a cop.   HA!   The dirty old sod doesn't believe he's done anything wrong!   It's amazing what some men will get off on!   In fact I can't believe I have to represent him - all I want to do is punch his stupid face.   Just shows, money talks.

18th December 1998

Party night.   Was only at the prison till lunch, but had masses of paperwork to do when I got back to the office.   Started getting ready for party at 5pm.   The bathroom on the knob's floor is amazing and about three times the size of our house!   The party was fab, which was no surprise since I was involved in the organization – if there's only one thing I can do, it's throw a good party!   I got a little drunk though and got plenty of stares in my sexy dress.
'You polish up quite well,' Nick said to me while we served ourselves to the lethal fruit punch.
'What, this old thing, I didn't get chance to look for something new with all the hours I have to put in at this place,' I said.

He smiled, puckered his lips at me then returned to the side of this strange, miserable looking woman I'd never seen before. The party went great then about 11pm, a very, *very* drunk Claudia, from 3rd floor, did a twirl on the dance floor and fell against the speaker, knocking it flying. That was the end of the disco and the good music. The DJ – somebody's nineteen year old son – couldn't get the speaker to work so the evening turned into a karaoke for piss-heads. I got dragged up to do a rendition of '*Down Town*' with Debbie and Pippa – at least the drink blocked it all out!!

25th December 1998

Christmas day was like no other. Santa left me some cash, a couple of tops, a *Top Shop* voucher and some chocolates; he left Sara more or less the same. The atmosphere in the house was horrid and me and Sara were banished to Gran's for day so that Mom and Dad could 'sort things out.' Gran had cooked a turkey and after helping our grandmother in the kitchen, Sara and I got pissed on sherry and Malibu (not in the same glass but with any mixer, though not keen on Malibu and prune juice!).
We brought home a doggy bag for our starving parents. Home atmosphere was slightly less hostile and was fortunately numbed by alcohol. Parents went out and we ate all the toffee pennies and strawberry creams from the tin of *Quality Street*, while we watched *Babe* and spent whole film deliberating about how they'd got the animals to talk!

30th December 1998

Diary, dear diary, I believe. I really, truly do believe. I believe that, overnight, my parents were abducted by aliens, had something done to their brains and then were returned to us. Never again will I doubt the existence of the little green men with big heads! They are NOT splitting up. IT'S A MIRACLE! And they are happy, happier than they have been in a long time and life is good, everything is good and, I'M NOT PISSED!
On the other hand, work's boring at the moment and sexy Nick's off

for the holidays – in fact loads of people are off – the place is really quiet.

Mandy phoned, I haven't spoken to her for ages – she's having a New Year's Eve party so me and Sara are going.

1st January 1999

My head feels like it's being ripped apart.   I'm never drinking again.   I know not to mix my drinks and what did I do?   Wine, champagne and Malibu.   God what a mix! Never again.   Sara pulled though, lucky cow.   Tony, the guy she's fancied from school - watch this space.   Going to Gran's for dinner so will need to sober up.

11th January 1999

Sara's gone back to uni – will her new found love survive the distance?

That crusty old, knicker watching toff got off with a warning – I CAN'T BELIEVE IT!!!   To add insult to injury, he wanted to buy me a present, I told him to sod off.

14th January 1999

I CAN'T BELIEVE IT!   Nick asked me out on a yellow sticky note.   I sent 'yes' back on a blue!

15th January 1999

Work was dead boring and Nick was out of the office all day. Hope he wasn't winding me up!

Things still running smoothly with mother and father – fingers crossed.

19th January 1999

Nick wasn't winding me up!   He called me into his office to discuss new case.
'How do you fancy going for a drink, Friday night?' he said.
'Yeah, that'd be great,' I said – tried to act cool, but, Yippee, dead exciting, looks like I finally have a boyfriend and potential sex life. Trauma, trauma, trauma, what will I wear?

22nd January 1999

Nick took me to *The Dog and Partridge*, near Hockley Heath.   Was a lovely place, really relaxing.   Was very careful what I drank as I didn't want to make a fool of myself.   Talked about work, food and favourite places.
'Where do you go drinking?' he said.
'Wherever,' I said, 'But only at weekends,' I lied.
He was the perfect gentleman, brought me home and didn't want to get in my knickers!   He drives a BMW and said I've got a nice figure – wait till you see me naked, matey!!!

29th January 1999

Nick took me for a curry – he knows how to treat a girl!   I had a prawn and spinach Balti, Nick had a chicken Bhuna.
'It's my favourite,' he said.
'This is my favourite,' I said.
We had a right laugh about the people at work.   Laughed so much I nearly pissed myself – had to rush to the bog.
Put lipstick on and shocked at reflection in mirror – BOLLOCKS! loads of spinach around teeth, hope Nick didn't notice, he didn't say anything so hopefully not . (Should have laughed with my mouth shut – is that possible?).

<u>2nd February 1999</u>

Sara's birthday – 20 today – she's catching me up!   Bought her a pair of jeans and a blouse and mom sent them in a parcel with their present – hope she's got them.   Looking forward to her coming home at the weekend, we'll probably go to the *Plough* – dad's favourite and we can catch up, see how her long-distance love life is going, maybe I'll tell her about Nick……?

<u>5th February 1999</u>

BOLLOCKS!   Sara can't get home – got some project she needs to hand in to lecturer on Monday.
BOLLOCKS twice – not seeing Nick this weekend either, he's got some knobs do that he can't get out of.   Looks like it's going to be a naff weekend.
God, must stop fucking swearing – I'll make it my belated New Year's resolution – good idea.

<u>7th February 1999</u>

Went to Gran's for dinner, with mom and dad – cottage pie week. Honestly, parents are like a couple of newly-weds – aren't they a bit old for all that?   Isn't it me and (currently non-existent) boyfriend who should be cuddling up on the settee and not ancient parents who should have some consideration for their off-spring?

<u>12th February 1999</u>

Nick took me to *The Old Barn* for a drink.   Have been seeing him for 3 weeks now but still no mention of sex.   Oh no, what if he doesn't fancy me and I fancy him to bits?   He could be shy – that's sweet, maybe he wants to be dominated, haha!   We've kissed loads and he's good at that, is he waiting for me to make the first move…..?

<u>13th February 1999</u>

We had a flutter of snow today and it's so bloody cold (oops! But technically, bloody isn't swearing, is it?)   I wish the summer would hurry up.

Mandy asked me to go to Spain with her this year.   I might go, unless me and Nick go somewhere (white sand, tropical beaches, a luxury yacht gently bobbing on a mill pond sea, eating oysters and peaches, drinking champagne and making love from dawn till dusk….)

Need to stop constantly thinking about boyfriend.   Victoria and Nicholas; Nicholas and Victoria; Vick and Nick; Nicky and Vicky! YUK!!!

I wonder how many Valentine cards I'll get.

<u>14th February 1999</u>

Two Valentine cards pushed through the front door, one was to dad from mom and the other was to mom from dad.   Nothing for me, but I refuse to swear about it.

<u>15th February 1999</u>

No sign of any Valentine cards on my desk when I got to work – boyfriend's obviously playing it cool.   Thought I'd remind him, sneaked up to his office and left mine on his desk.

'Thanks for the card,' he said.

'How do you know it was from me?   I didn't sign it,' I said.

'Saw you sneaking out of my office.'

'Oh.'

'Sorry, but I didn't think to get you one,' he said.

'It's ok.   It's just a joke really, a load of bollocks if you ask me,' I said.   (Oops, but mitigating circumstances).   I sulked for the rest of the day.

18th February 1999

NEWSFLASH!   How fab is this?   Dad had a call from someone he used to work with who was also injured by the same faulty machine and are suing.   The company has finally admitted liability and will be making compensation payments.   Dad needs to make a claim and he's asked his loyal and professional daughter to assist. He's really happy at the moment and he's taking me, mom and Gran out for a meal tonight, to celebrate.
I asked Nick to come but he said it was too short notice and he was busy.   Never mind, he can meet the future in-laws another time – don't want to scare him off before we've even shagged!

22nd February 1999

Nick asked me to go to a hotel with him for weekend!!!   Am sooo excited; a dirty weekend with my fella in some posh hotel.   Looks like I'm finally getting a sex life!
'I'm going to bring you something to wear, something special,' he said.
'Oh, ok,' I said.
'What size are you, 10?'
'On a good day, yes, though usually 10 – 12,' I said.
'You won't need to take much, just something for during the day and maybe something to wear if we go to dinner,' he said.
Jesus, (religious, so not strictly swearing), my mind's working overtime.   He's sooo kind, he's buying me something to wear, might even be a designer dress and what did he say, 'I won't need to take much' and 'If we go to dinner.'   We're going to be in bed ALL day and we're going to have room service –it's going to be sooo romantic.   Must sort out sexy underwear and MUST REMEMBER TO GET JONNIES!!!

25th February 1999

Weekend is still on.   To be honest, diary, I'm getting a bit nervous now, but looking forward to getting away from home for a couple of days and with handsome fella so all good!

Nick doesn't speak much at work.   I suppose it's difficult for him especially as he's one of the senior partners and I'm just junior staff. He leaves me lovely messages on sticky notes, though.

'Looking forward to our weekend,' he wrote, today.   He's so sweet and romantic, definitely got the best one of the partners.   I think I might buy a present to give to him at the hotel.

Will have to make sure I'm still with him next year, it's a leap year and I can propose – how cool is that?

27th February 1999

A very eventful weekend!!!

Met Nick at the end of our road.   He didn't want to come to my house, ah, I think he is shy.

The hotel was near Warwick, it was lovely.   It had a swimming pool and spa, beautician, everything and the food was delicious. When we got there, we walked round the grounds, holding hands and stopping every now and again for a snog, it was really romantic. There was a huge lake with ducks on it.   When it started to rain we went to the bar and had pre-lunch drinks.   I was starving and could feel the alcohol taking effect.   We ate soup, salmon with noodles and a delicious lemon cheesecake all washed down with a bottle of champagne.   Nick really knows how to show a girl a good time!

After lunch, we went back to the room.   Nick read the Guardian newspaper, I read my *Cosmo*.

'Have you digested your lunch?' he said.

'Yes,' I said and thought, 'This is it.'

Nick came over to me and kissed me passionately then said he was going to the car.   My heart was pounding as he left the room; I didn't know whether to strip off and get under the covers or put some sexy underwear on and lie across the top of the bed.   I decided to do neither in case he just wanted to go jogging.

Nick came back with a big leather gym bag.   I didn't think it looked like designer wear – was relieved that I hadn't undressed as he obviously wanted to go jogging or use the gym.

Nick took what looked like an extra-large school uniform out of the bag and laid it on the bed.   I was worried that he wanted me to put that on but then he took a grey shift-style dress from the bag and gave it to me.

'I like role play.   I like to be a naughty school boy and you are my teacher scolding me.   Is that ok?' he said.

I didn't know what to think; I didn't say anything and just stared.   HOW BLOODY WEIRD!

'I want you to be cross with me.   I want you to put me over this chair, expose my bottom and whack me with this spanker until my bottom is really red and I'm begging you to stop.   But don't stop, keep going for a few more minutes, but I don't want to bleed!' he said.

'Why?' I said.

'It's how I am, Victoria.   At work, I'm a very powerful man; I'm responsible for millions of pounds, people's lives, their futures and that of their family's are in my hands.   Sometimes I just want to be a carefree pupil again, sitting in the class, idolizing my teacher. Didn't you ever fancy your teacher?' he said.

'Yes I did, actually.   I fancied Mr Bowen, last year at seniors, he was dead sexy in his tight brown cords but I never wanted to whip him, or him me,' I said.

'The spanking is you having control over me, like a teacher controls her class.   You're the powerful one and I'm at your mercy; many men in positions of authority are like me.   Look, I'm sorry, Victoria, but it's what I enjoy.   Can we just give it a go?' he said.

I did what he wanted.   It was bloody strange but I thought what the hell.   I'm open to new experiences, I suppose.   I spanked his backside good and hard – he deserved it, didn't he?   I couldn't help but giggle while I was hitting him.   Afterwards, we made love and it was wonderful but I couldn't stop thinking about his unusual request.

We didn't go to dinner and had room service then stayed in bed watching old black and white movies.

28th February 1999

We made love again before breakfast.   I didn't have to dress up again and there was no mention of it - thank God.   Breakfast was a lovely buffet fry-up and I ate tons but it was really yummy.   Nick filled his plate once and didn't get up again – it was funny watching him grimace every time he sat down!   We had to check-out after breakfast which was a shame but we had half an hour in the bath in our room, beforehand – it was a huge bath - could have easily fitted another couple in - not that I'd entertain that idea!!!

Nick dropped me at the end of my road - don't know what he's worried about.
'I'm very grateful for your participation in our little game, I actually think that you're quite good at it, Victoria,' he said.
'I actually think I am,' I said.
'I trust that you will keep this between us and not broadcast it to all and sundry and in particular, the office,' he said.
'Do you honestly think that I'd want to tell anyone?' I said.
We kissed passionately then Nick went.
I spent the rest of the day thinking about my romantic AND WEIRD weekend with lover boy.   It's not that bad I suppose, I could get used to it.   I guess I'll have to, if I want to keep seeing Nick.

1st March 1999

March already!   Nick wasn't at work today and Molly was off sick. He didn't mention he wouldn't be in – hope I didn't hit him too hard and he's off with a sore arse (oops!).
On the subject of swearing, dad's introduced a swear box, it's sitting in the lounge, on the mantel piece and in full view.   It's got a huge sign on it - 50p for every swear word.   I accidently said 'Frig.'
'That'll cost you 50p,' dad said, shaking the box at me.
'I haven't sworn.   Frig's not swearing,' I said, but he wasn't interested in protestations.
He still wants me to help him out with his compensation - must chase that up, we haven't heard anything yet.

2nd March 1999

Had the strangest dream last night, had my own office and Nick Crawford, Steven Cavendish and Gerald Simspson were taking it in turns to come in and get spanked – God, so glad I'm sharing an office!

Molly's still off sick - someone said she's got shingles - she'll be off for ages.   I miss her - she's a good laugh.

Briefly glimpsed Nick today talking with the other knobs, God he's sexy.   He didn't come to see me though; he's obviously playing it cool, can't wait till we go out again.   Doesn't he realise what he's doing to me?   I WANT HIM, I WANT HIM!

Hope the weather gets better now spring's on its way.

5th March 1999

Nick's given me the cold shoulder all week – the little shit.   Well he can just sod off if he's moaning about something. And to think I played his stupid bloody game!

Swear box is costing me a fortune; I've put £3 in already this week. The more I try not to swear, the more I do.   So much for my belated New Year resolution!

Sara's home - study week.   She and Tony are going into town tonight.   I hate being stuck in on a Friday - I wonder if they'll let me tag along!

6th March 1999

Headache from hell.   Went to town with Sara but met up with Pippa and Debbie from work, ended up in *Ronnie Scott's*, with them.

Was hilarious –Pippa said someone found a pair of knickers and a mouldy sandwich behind the filing cabinet a couple of days ago, I didn't ask!!!!!

Dad's compo info came and of course he needed me to read it all straight away - couldn't wait for a while and give the *Paracetamol* time to kick in!

8th March 1999

Well it looks like it's over for me and Nick.   He hasn't spoken to me for ages and I've seen him around the office – obviously only after one thing.   Stuff him, though if I'd known he was going to dump me, I'd have spanked him harder.   I'll just have to put it down to experience.   A bit embarrassing though since we work at the same place.

Are all men complete bastards?   (Apart from dads that is).

10th March 1999

He's only asked me to go out with him on Friday - Nick that is. What a bloody tease!   Of course I said yes!!

12th March 1999

Nick took me to *The Dog and Partridge*, again.   The bastard's married.   They're separated but his wife wants to use me as the cause for the separation so she gets the house.   She's the miserable looking cow from the Christmas party – BITCH!   So that's it, another failed relationship.   God, what is it with me and men?

13th March 1999

Can't believe I've been dumped.   Feel lonely again and a bit of a prat for dressing up and doing that kinky sex thing for him.   Sorry diary but too down in the dumps to tell you anything else.

14th March 1999

Parents in a good mood today and took us to *The Plough* for a meal as Sara's going back to Manchester on Tuesday.   Was really good

but made a bit of a pig of myself - their puddings are sooo delish.
Dreading going to work tomorrow and seeing that dickhead.

15th March 1999

No sign of dickhead - thank God.

16th March 1999

'Mr Crawford's out of the office all week for personal reasons.
Any problems need to be directed to Steven Cavendish or David
Simpson,' Debbie said.   Personal reasons!   Well we all know what
that's about don't we?   Or at least, I know, even if no-one else does
– I'll have to be really careful what I say!
Does the dickhead still deserve my discretion?

17th March 1999

Down in the dumps today, heartbreak is horrid, trying to keep
reminding myself that we didn't see that much of each other anyway
so wasn't full blown love affair.
Explains why he didn't want to meet my parents or pick me up from
the house when we went away - left me to struggle down the road
with my suitcase - TOSSER!   I HATE MEN! HATE 'EM!!!
Didn't feel up to going to the St Patrick's Day party with Mandy and
Julia – told them I wasn't well – I hate lying to my friends - that's
his fault – TOSSER TWICE!!!!!!

24th March 1999

OH MY BLOODY GOD – sorry but I have to swear!   Got called

into dickhead's office today - that bloody wife of his has been causing trouble and they've given me the frigging sack!!! That stupid tosser didn't even stick up for me, not once! Couldn't even look me in the eye. They're giving me 4 months' wages and references for future jobs. I can't believe it. I haven't even completed a year there.
Put £2 in swear box.

29th March 1999

Got up after nine and didn't rush through the bathroom.
'No work today?' dad asked.
'Don't work there anymore, it didn't work out,' I said.
'They given you the push, have they? I bet you swore at your boss, didn't you?' he said (a bit too judgmentally for my liking).
'No, I didn't actually, they were cutting back, last in, first out,' I said.
'Don't go wasting that degree,' he said.
'I won't,' I said.
'Something will turn up,' mom said.
Relieved the inquisition wasn't as bad as I thought it would be – didn't have to tell great stinking lies to family.

14th April 1999

Working part time in a pet shop – some friend of dad's knows the owner's dad. Cleaning out stinky cages and filling up feed trays, the place stinks of poo and grain and I've never felt so riffy in my life (even when I helped my snobby school friend, Davina, clean out her pony's stable, in Hampton-in-Arden). It's a bit of a come down really, but it will do, for now. Travis (the owner) thinks I'm so stupid that I don't know he's standing behind me staring at my bum when I'm cleaning the lower cages – what a perv! Some customers are ok, but I think most of them belong in a cage themselves.

<u>16th April 1999</u>

Pervy boss asked me out for a drink (surprise surprise).
'How desperate do you think I am?' I said.
'You should think yourself lucky working here, many girls like you would give their right arm to work here with me,' he said.
'They wouldn't be able to clean out many shitty cages with only one arm,' I said.

<u>6th May 1999</u>

Mandy got me a waitressing job covering weddings at her hotel.
Thank God, sooo glad to get out of that stinky pet shop.

<u>15th May 1999</u>

First day at waitressing job, was v nervous and v embarrassed when I dropped the spuds in some guys' lap. 'Fucking idiot,' he said. Was tempted to stick the fork in his head. 'Sorry,' I said.

<u>20th May 1999</u>

Getting to be a dab-hand at this waitressing lark – the money's crap but the tips are good.

<u>29th May 1999</u>

Snogged the best man today, handsome as hell, (and didn't he know it!) I had to be careful though as working. 'What is it that a best man's so good at?' I said. 'What do you think?' he said. My legs went to jelly. He's got my phone number. He said his name's Danny.

Never heard squat from Danny – no surprise there - all men ARE Bastards!   Got promoted though - now behind the bar.   It's a good laugh, work with a girl called Charlotte and a guy called Spencer, nice enough, but I think he's gay.

10th June 1999

Mom and Dad left the house early to go on a coach trip to Weston-Super-Mare.
I didn't even hear them go.   I had a lie-in and a soak in the bath.
Had just finished crossword when the door knocked.   It was only bloody NICK SODDING CRAWFORD!!!
'You've got a nerve,' I said.
'Hear me out,' he said, in his stuck up way.
So I invited him in for a cup of tea.   He waited till my mouth was full of digestive biscuits then only asked me to play that stupid game with him again.
'Are you fucking joking?' I said, trying to keep the crumbs in my mouth.
'I have needs,' he said.   'I'm willing to pay you £50.'
'Fifty fucking quid for that?' I said.
'Yes,' he said.
'What about your wife?'
'She won't indulge,' he said.
'So you thought you'd come to me?'
'Yes.   What if I increase it to £80,' he said.
'And what about afterwards?' I said; he frowned.   'Afterwards, you, me, the hotel room?'
'Ah that.   Afterwards, I get dressed and leave, there can be nothing more, Victoria.   This is purely a business transaction,' he said.
'Alright, you're on,' I said.   He had his bag with him; our costumes were in it – of course.
I took him to my bedroom.
'I like your room,' he said.
'Good, 'cus you're going to feel some bad pain in it,' I said.
'Splendid,' he said.

I beat his backside extra hard – well he deserved it, didn't he?
Thought he would stop me, but he didn't – I actually think he liked
it.   I kept going for ten minutes – his backside was really red, like
the monkeys in the zoo.   I got tired and had to quit.
'Thank you,' he said.   He went into the bathroom for ages.   I
thought he was dead.   When he came out, he looked happy.   He
gave me eighty quid and kissed me on the head then went.
Put a fiver in the swear box for my swear crimes, after all, swearing
with food in one's mouth must be the height of bad manners!

Mom and dad came home like a pair of newly-weds – all cheerful
and lovey dovey.   They enjoyed themselves so much they'd booked
a week there, in July!

11th June 1999

Couldn't face mom's cheese flan so took her and dad to the *Three
Horseshoes* for dinner.   Dad was suspicious.
'I've been saving my tips,' I said.
'Can't see you earning any,' he said.   He stopped going on about it
when his steak came.   At least mom was grateful. (Don't think she
fancied her flan either!)

17th June 1999

Nick 'naughty boy' Crawford came round.   Mom answered the
door.   I watched him saunter up the path with his gym bag.   Jeez,
does he think I've got nothing better to do?
'Some chap selling food mixers,' mom said.
'Just popping out,' I said.
Ran down road and caught Nick as he was just getting into his car.
Have arranged rendezvous for next Tuesday when mom and dad are
out for lunch.

22nd June 1999

Nick knocked door seconds after mom and dad left – must've been waiting for them to go! Same scenario – my room, teacher gives naughty school boy good spanking then naughty schoolboy goes in bathroom to die.

I felt a bit brave, 'I hope you're not hiding in there, Nicholas Crawford,' I said.

'No Miss, just refreshing myself,' he said.

He gave me an extra 20 quid for the adlib – said it really turned him on! Re-booked for 24th at 10 am (mom and dad will be out, it's Uncle Jack's birthday).

24th June 1999

10.01 exactly – Jeez, he's eager! Answered the door with bright red lipstick, dark-rimmed spectacles and a stern look.

'Fuck me, Miss Golightly, you look hot,' he said.

'Mm, if only I could,' I thought. 'Do not speak to your teacher in that manner,' I said. 'In fact, do not speak to me at all and get upstairs.'

Got changed and put on new high heeled shoes – picked up specs and shoes from bargain basket at *Top Shop*. 'Nick Crawford, you have let me down,' I said.

'Sorry Miss,' he said.

'And you've let yourself down,' I said.

'Sorry Miss,' he said.

'For that, you will be punished,' I said.

'Yes Miss,' he said.

Whacked his arse really hard then he went into the bathroom. He gave me an extra 50 quid for the shoes and specs. I think I'm getting quite good at this!

Went to *The Plough* tonight with mom, dad, Uncle Jack, Auntie Jemma and Grandma. I had breaded mushrooms, tuna steaks, vanilla cheesecake and few glasses of Chardonnay, to wash it down – was a good night.

25th June 1999

Headache from hell and had to work – didn't even drink that much. They were a waitress down so I had to come from behind the bar. Spoilt little brat put mashed potato in my apron pocket. Lecherous groom and some old sod kept eyeing me up – who do they think they are? They'd soon think again if I spanked their arses till they were red like the monkeys in the zoo!
Sara's coming home next week.

5th July 1999

Sara and Tony have split up! Spent the morning consoling sister. Sister spent the morning saying 'shit.' Dad spent the morning shaking swear box at distraught daughter. I actually think she may have put more cash in that box than I have. Never seems to fill up though. Will have to check with parents as to whereabouts of fines.

6th July 1999

Spent the day shopping with Sara, had to go to Sutton Coldfield though, to ensure no chance of bumping into Tony. God, just imagine if he'd thought the same thing and gone to Sutton too! Ha, don't be a cruel and wicked sister!! Sara bought a strange blue/black dress that I'd never be seen dead in and wasn't sure she really wanted it – probably comfort buying. I picked up a black pencil skirt with a zip up the back – thought it would probably come in handy.
Went to *The Bull's Head* after shopping trip. Sara got drunk then cried all the way home. All men are BASTARDS, Sara. I hope she gets over this soon.

10th July 1999

Waved mom, dad and Sara off for their week in Weston-Super-Mare. Was looking forward to house-sitting with sister, but, oh well – hooray – house to myself for a whole week.
Tony phoned, wanted to speak to Sara. 'Sod off, you little shit,' I

said and added 'bastard' on account of dad's absence.   Checked swear box for recording equipment then said, 'Fuck, shit, bollocks,' to swear box.   Shook the box, still no fuller than before, must check with parents as to whereabouts of fines.

Tony phoned again – told him Sara's gone on a *Club 18 – 30* holiday and won't be back for two weeks, Tony said, 'Oh,' and put the phone down.

Thought I might go on a *Club 18-30* holiday, myself but then remembered Mandy hadn't said anything about our holiday proposal.

Phoned Mandy, she's well but had forgotten about holiday idea. 'Can't go anyway as I'm saving for my own place,' she said.

'Oh, okay,' I said, but was quite disappointed.

11th July 1999

Went to Grandma's for dinner, it's cottage pie week.   Uncle Jack popped in with the newspapers and stayed for a cup of tea.   After dinner, Grandma got the cards out and we played *Sevens* and *Old Maid*.   I had two Sherries with Gran then came home.   Got an appointment with Nick in the morning, he said he'd be round early – God, I hope he's not too bloody early.

12th July 1999

9.31 am, knock at front door.   Answered door in new pencil skirt, heels, specs, red lipstick and stern look.   Frigging postman!   Had a parcel for next door.

'They're at work,' I said.

'Can you take it?' postman said.

'Can you?' I thought.

9.45 am, knock at front door, looked out of window to check visitor, two men, one was Nick Crawford, I didn't know the other.   Frig – no time to change.   Rubbed off lipstick, removed heels and specs, answered door with a smile.

'This is Ian,' Nick said.

'Hi, Ian,' I said.

'Hi,' Ian said.

'Ian is like me,' Nick said.   'He likes the things I like; he's a naughty schoolboy too.   I've told him you're very discreet.'

'Oh, I see,' I said and made a hundred and fifty quid.

*****

18th March 2000

Have hangover from hell from last night's St Patrick's Day party, but not all bad as met lovely Niall.   Hope I wasn't too drunk and made complete prat of myself but he seemed keen.   Oh well, will just have to wait for phone call!

21st March 2000

New guy, Crispin, turned up, wanted 'Naughty Boy' treatment, another 'referral.'   Obviously word's getting around.   Sent him packing as mom and dad at home.   Told him to come back Thursday as parents will be out.

They're taking Gran for a hospital appointment – hope she's okay.

22nd March 2000

Need to look for my own place as parents are starting to get annoying.

'Are you selling drugs?' dad asked.

'What?' I said.

'You must be, to fund your lifestyle, bar work and waitressing doesn't pay that much.'

If ever I needed to swear, but I didn't, I kept my cool.   'What about your law degree, when are you going to get a proper job?' he said.

'I like waitressing and the tips are good and if I'm short of a few

quid, I raid the swear box,' I said.
'Thought so,' he said.
'As if, what do you do with the cash?' I said.
'Put it in the housekeeping,' mom said.
'I'm going to my room to bag some pills, got loads of orders to meet,' I said.

23rd March 2000

Crispin arrived at 11 am.   Very particular, keeps underpants on and sets timer, likes exactly three minutes of spanking.   Doesn't use the bathroom and pays 75 quid.   High up in banking, or something like that, I think.   What is it about big knobs and spanking?
Niall phoned tonight – yippee!   We're going out on Saturday – yippee!
Gran's okay, got tablets for her waterworks – good on ya, Gran.

25th March 2000

Sara and Tony are back together, ah, he went up to see her at uni. Sara said she's staying in Manchester, Tony said he's going up there to live, how romantic - hope Niall's as romantic as that.
Must go and get ready for date.

26th March 2000

Couldn't find new dress for date with Niall, searched very overcrowded wardrobe – twice, was forced to wear leggings and *Monsoon* top – looked nice anyway.   Went to O'Neill's in town.
'What job do you do?' he said.
'Waitressing and bar work,' I said.
'Well that's a fine occupation,' he said.
'What about spanking?' I thought.   Niall works for the council.
'Good luck with that,' I said.

He's taking me for a meal next week.   'Let someone wait on you for a change,' he said.
'How kind,' I thought.

27th March 2000

Found my new dress in mom's wardrobe – what the frig was it doing there?
'I haven't worn it,' mom said.
'Why was it in there then?' I said.
'Because you hadn't the space in yours, oh really, Victoria,' she said.
Must sort out wardrobe AND stop swearing AND do client list.

8th April 2000

Shock horror!!! Dad's got a job, well not horror, really, but definitely a shock.   Starts after Easter – an admin job at a recruitment office, well done dad.
Sara came home today.

9th April 2000

Everybody round at ours.   Me, mom and Sara in kitchen all morning making buffet.   Big celebration for dad's job.   Uncle Jack, Auntie Jemma, Grandma, Tony, Mandy and Jake (her boyfriend – who just happens to be taking her on *our* holiday to Spain) and of course the lovely Niall, all squeezed into our tiny living room.   Plenty of food and plenty of wine - was a good day.
Niall kept stroking my bum – he's really hot, can't wait to get him in the sack.   Can't tell him about the spanking, not yet, anyway.

15th April 2000

Sara and Tony went to see Tony's Mom.   Mom and dad went to the shops to get dad kitted out for work.   Niall came round and we spent the morning in bed, made love three times!   Was knackering - didn't think I'd ever walk again.   He's a dead nice, straightforward guy with no kinky role play.   Can't wait till we get the house to ourselves again – will definitely have to look for a place – definitely need privacy!!!!!

22nd April 2000

Sara went back to Manchester, Tony went with her – they're going to look for a place together – can't believe she's nearly finished uni!

25th April 2000

Dad loves his job (though only first day.)   He took mom out for a meal.   Alexander called round for a quick wank (oops) spank.
Felt guilty about lying to Niall but Alexander's £50 payment made me feel better.

26th April 2000

Started flat hunting – why is everything so frigging expensive?
Mom met dad for lunch which gave me chance to do Sir Brendan.
Laddered another pair of stockings on his damn nails – why does he insist on stroking my leg while I spank him?   Never mind, he pays well - £75.
Must remember to do client list, need to be professional – a who's who of spankees!!!

12th May 2000

Just found diary in bottom of box marked 'KITCHEN,' wondered where it had got to!!
Today was a momentous occasion, I moved into my own flat.   My

new address is: **First Floor Flat, 19 Berryfield Road, Tyseley.**
Niall helped me move, he took the day off work – it must be love!
Unpacked half of the boxes then made love on the lounge floor
cushions – he's so romantic.   Must get some furniture!!!

14th May 2000

Decided to plan a flat-warming party for Friday 26th May – can't
wait.

16th May 2000

Nick and Sir Brendan, today (not at the same time!) - made 150
quid.   Will invest in some new equipment, have decided to make
spare bedroom into mock classroom – it's great having my own
space!!!

25th May 2000

Struggled home with drinks for the party and leatherwear, chains and
whips for the classroom.
Neighbour offered to help so I gave him the bag with the kinky stuff
in!
Life would be much easier with a car – must learn to drive!!

26th May 2000

Flat warming party – loads of people came, there were quite a few I
didn't know – thanks to Rick the hippy, from the downstairs flat -
he's okay though and his mates were okay too, (didn't need to get
the whip out to get rid of them!).   Mom and dad came, briefly.
'Music's too loud and there's nowhere to sit,' Dad said.
'There's a bed settee in the spare room,' I said.

'Why've you got so many kitchen rolls in there?' he said.
'For all the spillages, I get lots and they're dead absorbent,' I said.
'Are you looking after yourself and eating properly?' Mom said.
'I see you nearly every day, Mom,' I said and then they left.
Nick sent champagne but didn't attend.   Sara and Tony couldn't make it; they'd gone to Majorca for the week.   Mandy popped in for a quick orange juice then had to go to work.
I drank too much champagne.   Niall asked me about the spare room.
'Why does your second bedroom resemble a classroom?' he said.
'It's the spanking room,' I said and then my drunken brain couldn't stop the words flying out of my big gob – he didn't look impressed and left.

27th May 2000

Pounding headache and loads of cleaning up to do – alone as stroppy boyfriend pissed off last night.   God, I hope he calls, then I can tell him I was joking, it's really my study room – should I be lying to my boyfriend?
Phone rang – thought it was Niall.   It was mom, she and dad came round with the hoover and helped me clear up – I have lovely parents!

4th June 2000

Still no word from Niall, can't believe I'm such a stupid, drunken, big mouth prat.   I hate not having a boyfriend.

5th June 2000

Sorry diary, too depressed to write.

5th July 2000

New client – Ronald Stevenson the third.   Knew his face but couldn't place it.

"I believe you are in the business of satisfying gentlemen with particular tastes,' he said.   'Maybe,' I said.

'I wonder if you would be prepared to expose your undergarments to me for which you will receive very generous remuneration,' he said.

That's where I knew his face from – he's that crusty old toff who got caught looking at women's knickers.

'I represented you,' I said.

'You did, and very well too.   I had no complaints, though I think you are more cut out for this line of work, young lady,' he said.

It's easy, he sits at a desk, I bend over and he lifts the hem of my dress with a pencil and peeks at my panties.   I look shocked and spank him for his cheek then he gives me £50!

Bet Nick sent him my way – cheeky sod!!!

17ᵗʰ July 2000

Never heard from Niall again, oh well, stuff him, single minded dickhead – still, it was good while it lasted – I am a bit sad though, don't like not having a boyfriend.

Another new client today, Montgomery Drewton, (quite high up in the NHS, I think).   Likes to be tied up with leather straps and have balls whipped – ouch!   Didn't want to be too rough so went gently.

'Oh, Miss Golightly, don't go lightly,' he said.   So I didn't!!

Montgomery paid me £100 and re-booked for next month.

Made a sign for naughty room door: **MISS DON'T GOLIGHTLY   CLASS 2.**

*****

13ᵗʰ March 2013

Crapping crappiness, something terrible's happened.   Had to go out for a new whip (and other equipment) but also my turn to visit Grandma.

'Are you sure you don't mind coming with me, Gran?' I said.

'Of course I don't.   I'll wait while you're getting your shopping, then we'll go and get some lunch, my treat,' she said.

But she didn't wait, did she?   I left her on the wall outside *Ann Summers*, and when I came out, there was no sign of her.   I searched the whole of Solihull town centre, looked on every floor of her favourite – *Marks and Spencer* – but couldn't find her.

Tried her on her mobile (don't think she can hear it, let alone know how to answer it!) and got a right bollocking when I confessed to mom and dad.

'How did you manage to lose your Grandmother?' dad said.

'I didn't lose her, she wandered off when I was in the underwear shop,' I said.

'Why didn't you take her in the underwear shop with you?' mom said.

'She didn't want to come in, she wanted to sit on the wall outside,' I said.

Dad and mom went to Gran's at 9pm, there was no sign of her and she still wasn't answering her phone.

14th March2013

Nobody's speaking to me and Gran's still missing.   Mom's been phoning round hospitals and OAP homes.   I feel really shit.

15th March 2013

Dad and mom have been to police to report Gran as missing.   Dad's been given special leave from work.   Sara phoned and told me I was stupid – as if I need her to tell me that.

16th March 2013

Still no sign of Gran.   At least dishing out pain to clients takes my mind off it all – for a while anyway.

17th March 2013

Still no sign of Gran.   Have visions of notorious gang, snatching pensioners from the street and selling them on to ruthless gang masters who force them into slave labour.   Parents and sister still hate me.

19th March 2013

Didn't think it could get any worse, but it did.   Still no sign of grandmother and now sister has gone into early labour with second child – baby not due till mid April.   Now I'm really in the dog house.
Where the hell is Gran?   If only there was some news.

20th March 2013

Dominic Peter was born at 4.15am – mother and baby are doing fine – thank God.   Briefly wondered if she'd named him after me?
Still no sign of Gran, though.

22nd March 2013

Dear diary, you'll never guess who's back.   YES, GRANDMOTHER!!!   Turned up at about 9pm last night.   Dad, mom and I were in her lounge – looking for clues – when she strolled in, like she'd just come back from the corner shop.
'Where've you been, Mom?' dad said.
'On my holidays,' she said.
'Where?   With who?' mom said.

'Rosie Danks, an old bingo friend, I haven't seen her for ages. Her husband died a few years ago but she's got herself a toy boy now,' she said.

'We were worried about you, Mom.' dad said.

'You needn't have been,' Gran said.

'Victoria was very irresponsible, leaving you alone like that,' mom said.

'She's a grown woman, not a toddler,' I said.

'Don't be daft, Victoria did me a favour. If she hadn't left me outside that kinky shop, I'd never have seen my old friend. I knew our Vicky would be in there for a while, so Horace, that's the toy boy's name, Rosie and I went for a coffee in that expensive coffee place. Rosie told me about the trip they were taking and they invited me along. I didn't have time to wait for Vicky so I packed a few things then we went touring round England. We've stayed at some lovely places, I've paddled in the sea and watched the sun go down; I've had a wonderful time,' Gran said.

'We filed a missing persons report,' mom said.

'I'm sorry, I was having such a good time, I forgot to phone you, that's all,' Gran said.

'As long as you're okay, Gran?' I said.

'I am, chick, and I might even get myself a toy boy,' Gran said.

24th March 2013

Grandma celebrated her return by inviting us all round to dinner – it's cottage pie week.

17th April 2013

Found three sodding grey hairs – THREE!!! – it's from all the stress last month, when Gran did her disappearing act. At least parents and sister are talking to me again.

Briefly wondered if parents would send out a search party if I disappeared for a week or more and decided, probably not.

18th April 2013

Starting to develop fixation on frigging grey hairs, can't stop looking at them and strong desire to tug them out. Am well aware that for each one I pull out, two grow back – then I'd have six of the buggers. I'm 38, aren't I too young for grey hair?

19th April 2013

Have gone blonde and quite like the new me. Ian said he feels like he's being spanked by *Marilyn Monroe*.
'Well, when it comes to the *Monkey Business*, don't *Gentlemen Prefer Blondes?*' I said. He laughed and gave me £20 bonus.
Was tempted to mention *The Misfits*, but thought I'd better not push my luck.
Dad and mom are coming for tea, tomorrow - we're one big happy family again – hoorah! Wish the weather was a bit warmer; I could just do a ham salad, save the hassle of cooking.
Must tidy up flat. Can't help but keep looking at new hair.

20th April 2013

Re-arranged naughty room and hidden door sign – parents still believe it's a study (with spare bed). Wonder what they'd think if they knew! Cooked sausage and mash, went ok till dad started interrogation.
'When are you going to put that law degree to good use?' he asked.
'Don't know, didn't work too good last time,' I said.
'Are you sure you didn't upset someone?' mom said.
'What do you mean?' I said.
'You always were hot-headed,' dad said.
'Did you enjoy the sausage and mash?' I said.

'It was lovely, dear,' mom said.
'Cooking was never your thing,' dad said.
They went home at nine o'clock.

27th April 2013

Sara visited with Georgia and baby Dominic – who's dead cute.
'Did you name him after me?' I said.
'No, of course we didn't.   He's named after some distant cousin of Tony's and it was the name that appeared on both of our lists,' she said.
Sara and her brood are staying with parents for a few days and I think having a toddler around the house is a bit much for dad.
'I could make some space for you here,' I said.
'I don't want my children sleeping in the room of pain,' she said.
I'm glad she knows about my business and I'm glad she's ok about it.   She stayed for lunch then Georgia got tired and she ran out of bibs for an ever-vomiting, Dominic.
Going to parents tomorrow (me, that is, not Sara who's already there).

28th April 2013

Met Sara and kids in park.   I pushed Georgia on swings while sis flashed breasts to everybody and fed her ever-hungry baby.   Briefly wondered if I'll ever have a baby but as I haven't even got a boyfriend, that's highly unlikely – certainly don't fancy the idea of donor sperm, knowing my luck, I'd end up with a kid like *Chucky,* neither am I desperate enough to start squeezing out the kitchen roll!!!
Mom cooked a huge roast dinner.   The visit to the park sent both kids to sleep.   Georgia was spark out on the settee and Dominic, who'd gorged on Sara's enormous boobs, fell asleep in the pram.
We sat round the table, just like the old days.
'Are you a lesbian?' dad said.   I nearly choked on my roast potato.
'What?' I said.

'Well you haven't got a boyfriend, have you? I can't remember the last time I saw you with a young man,' he said.

'That doesn't make her a lesbian,' Sara said.

'I've had a few boyfriends. They just don't stick around long,' I said.

'Probably because you're a lesbian,' dad said.

'I'm not a lesbian, I'm a dominatrix, I'm Miss Don't Golightly,' I wanted to say, but didn't.

'I'm not a lesbian, I just haven't met Mr Right, yet, that's all,' I said.

'You need to get out more, love,' mom said.

'And what about that law degree? All that hard work for nothing, a part time job, here and there, you should be settled down by now, could even have made partner,' dad said.

Sara and I washed up, dad fell asleep on the tiny part of the settee, not occupied by Georgia and mom changed Dominic's stinky nappy.

29th April 2013

Sara (and brood) going back to Manchester. Didn't sleep very well, things on mind. Do I need a boyfriend in life? Do I want to be alone and grow old alone? Will I still be able to lift a whip when I'm old and wrinkly? Perhaps I should stop providing kinky pain services and look for proper job, maybe if doing regular (normal, boring, tedious, mind-numbing) job, boyfriend will come along.

Went to parent's to see Sara off. Mom was feeding *Malted Milk* biscuits to Georgia and greedy Dominic was hanging from Sara's breast. If only I had someone hanging from my breast, though preferably a male around my age and definitely before breasts start heading south. Sister and kids went at one o'clock. I didn't hang around at family home - went to *Costa* and had a double espresso. Landlord came for the rent and his monthly visit to room of pain – at least it keeps the rent down.

30th April 2013

God, last day of April. Weather's still crap. When the fuck's the spring going to come.   Have decided, no more procrastinating, will start looking for law job, will not let spankees down, can do both. Law work Monday to Friday and spanking job at weekends – good – everybody happy.

ALSO, must stop swearing – not a good impression and need to be professional.

1st May 2013

Must sort out phoning round spanking clients to inform them of new arrangements – good idea to start now, will have new routine in place before new job starts.

Client List

Nick Crawford - June 1999: naughty schoolboy, likes to dress up and receive a good spanking (with leather spanker).   Weekly appointments, usually Thursday evening.   Payment varies, (I allow this as ex-lover) plus gifts.

Ian (don't know last name and have never asked) - July 1999: naughty schoolboy, likes to dress up and likes a good spanking (with spanker or plastic rule – never wooden).   Weekly appointments, Saturday morning (usually).   Payment varies, (I allow this as cute old man).

Sir Brendan - November 1999 – tall and skinny, looks like he needs a good meal: likes me to wear stockings and likes to stroke my leg during spanking (with hand or whip).   Fortnightly appointments, usually Tuesday mornings.   Payment £40 plus case of wine.

Crispin - March 2000: naughty boy (not school), likes to keep underpants on and sets timer for exactly 3 mins.   Fortnightly appointments, by phone arrangement.   Payment £75.

Alexander - April 2000: always stressed and rushing – doesn't have time for dressing up - likes a quick spank.   Weekly/twice weekly appointments by phone arrangement.   Payment £50.

Ronald Stevenson the third - July 2000: Old toff from lawyer days – likes to look at knickers and get spanked for doing so.   Payment £50 plus gifts.   Weekly appointments.

Montgomery Drewton - July 2000: strips off and likes me to wear leather, tied up with leather straps and have balls whipped. Monthly appointment by phone arrangement.   Payment £100.

Roger Carlingson - January 2003: likes to be chained (naked) and have stiletto heel in buttocks.   Fortnightly appointments arranged by text. Payment £50

Jefferson Whiting - June 2006: likes to be naughty schoolboy and get spanked.   Weekly appointments arranged by text.   Payment £40.

17th July 2013

HOLY CRAP, WOW!!!   Fantastic news – have got an interview for Weston and Weston Law Firm!   Feel really positive – good company to go for.   Aware that Nick has pulled a few strings but, hey, what are friends for other than spanking?!
Also aware that Nick's visited slightly more often since his ugly wife left him, and not just for a spank.   It seems that I'm seeing more of his face than his backside, these days!   Anyway, mustn't read too much into it and concentrate on impending interview – 11.15 am, Tuesday 6th August – will need to go into town and get an interview suit.   Feel really optimistic about this one……

THE END

Printed in Great Britain
by Amazon

30953609R00029